Michael Rose

HORN ON HOLIDAY

Nine easy pieces for horn in F
with piano accompaniment

ABRSM

Published by ABRSM (Publishing) Ltd, a wholly owned subsidiary of ABRSM
Printed in England by Caligraving Ltd, Thetford, Norfolk, on materials from sustainable sources
Reprinted in 2018

For Catherine

HORN ON HOLIDAY
Norwegian Holiday

MICHAEL ROSE

© 1992 by The Associated Board of the Royal Schools of Music.   AB 2295

CODA

D.S. to ⊕ and then to Coda

Holiday in Vienna

Holiday in Scotland

6

Swiss Holiday

D.S. al Fine

Caribbean Holiday

Poco allegro – lightly (♩ = 126)

For Catherine

HORN ON HOLIDAY

Norwegian Holiday

HORN in F

MICHAEL ROSE

© 1992 by The Associated Board of the Royal Schools of Music.   AB 2295

Holiday in Vienna

In the style of a Viennese waltz (𝅗𝅥. = 52)

Holiday in Scotland

Moderato – heavily (𝅘𝅥 = 84–88)

Swiss Holiday

Caribbean Holiday

Poco allegro – lightly (♩ = 126)

Holiday on the River

Russian Winter Holiday

Holiday in Israel

Spanish Holiday

D.S. to ⊕ and then to Coda

Holiday on the River

Russian Winter Holiday

Holiday in Israel

Spanish Holiday

D.S. to ⊕ and then to Coda

CODA